When Pioneer Wagons Rumbled West

When Pioneer Wagons Rumbled West

Written by Christine Graham

Illustrated by Sherry Meidell

Shadow Mountain, Salt Lake City, Utah

To Fred

CLG

To Grandma Linnie Burt

SLM

SHADOW MOUNTAIN®

Text ©1997 Christine Graham   Illustrations ©1997 Sherry Meidell

Shadow Mountain is a registered trademark of Deseret Book Company.

Library of Congress Cataloging-in-Publication Data

Graham, Christine, 1952–
When pioneer wagons rumbled west / text by Christine Graham ;
illustrations by Sherry Meidell.
p.   cm.
Summary: As pioneers endure the difficult journey over rivers,
through the dust, and across mountains, they turn to God for help.
ISBN 1-57345-272-6 (hb)
[1. Overland journeys to the Pacific—Fiction.   2. Frontier and
pioneer life—Fiction.   3. Christian life—Fiction.]
I. Meidell, Sherry, ill.   II. Title.
PZ7.G751673Wh   1997
[E]—dc21   97-15210
                                                                      CIP
                                                                       AC

Printed in Mexico
10   9   8   7   6   5   4   3   2   1

18961

When pioneer wagons rumbled west

The pioneers looked back at gardens,
Cabins,
Families,
And asked for God's help.

When their wagons crossed stream after stream
The pioneers splashed over sandbanks,
Swam through whirlpools,
Pulled oxen from mud,
And prayed as they pulled.

When their wagons stirred clouds of dust
The pioneers coughed, choked,
Squinted,
Wiped their faces,
And prayed in their hearts.

When their wagons stopped for rest
The pioneers found grass for the oxen,
Washed clothes,
Repaired wagons,
And asked for God's help.

When their wagons met travelers east
The pioneers found paper,
Wrote to their families
In tiny, crowded writing,
And asked for their prayers.

When their wagons sloshed through rains
The pioneers dripped,
Slipped,
Slogged on anyhow,
And prayed with each step.

When their wagons stopped for Sabbaths
The pioneers preached,
Sang,
Rested,
And asked for God's help.

When their wagons circled at day's end
The pioneers cared for their cattle,
Gathered buffalo chips,
Cooked beans and salt pork,
And prayed to have strength.

When their wagons stood above flickering campfires
The pioneers read,
Danced,
Laid out their bedding,
And prayed for good rest.

When their wagons carried the sick
The pioneers went on anyway,
Hoped for health,
Worried with faith,
And asked for God's help.

When their wagons came to swift, muddy rivers
The pioneers took out their tools,
Built strong rafts,
Ferried wagons,
And prayed as they worked.

When their wagons climbed steep mountains
The pioneers pushed,
Pulled,
Lightened their loads,
And prayed as they toiled.

When their wagons went down mountains
The pioneers moved the rocks,
Locked the wheels,
Dragged log brakes,
And asked for God's help.

When their wagons reached the valley
The pioneers unpacked their plows,
Got out their seeds,
Began to plant,
And thanked God for his help.